James Stevenson
Will You Please Feed Our Cat?

📖 GREENWILLOW BOOKS, NEW YORK

FOR LIZ DARHANSOFF

Black pen and watercolor paints
were used to prepare the full-color art.
The typeface is Clearface.

Library of Congress
Cataloging-in-Publication Data
Stevenson, James, (date)
Will you please feed our cat?
Summary:
When Mary Ann and Louie complain
about the troubles they are having
taking care of a neighbor's dog,
Grandpa remembers the time he and
his brother took care of their
neighbors' many pets and plants.
[1. Pets—Fiction.
2. Grandfathers—Fiction.
3. Cartoons and comics]   I. Title.
PZ7.S84748Wil 1987   [E]   86-11927
ISBN 0-688-06847-2
ISBN 0-688-06848-0 (lib. bdg.)

GEE, GRANDPA---ALL WE HAVE TO CARE FOR IS ONE DOG.

YOU'RE RATHER LUCKY...

HOW DID YOU DO IT ALL, GRANDPA?

"Well, the first day Wainey and I divided up the work.

...THEN YOU FEED THE FISH, WAINEY, I'LL FEED THE TURTLE, YOU CAN FEED THE CAT, I'LL FEED THE PARAKEET, YOU FEED THE GERBILS---AND DON'T FORGET TO CLOSE THAT SCREEN DOOR!

YUMP.

We explored the house..."

"I decided it would be quicker if I did all the feeding myself."

"I filled the watering can, but all I found was…

The greenhouse was enormous.

We watered flowers all day."

"We took lots of cups and string to the neighbors.

We filled the cups with pet food and hung them over the cages.

Then we threw one string
back to our house.

After that, all I had to do
was pull the string . . .

and all the animals got fed!"

"The cat was playing with the strings, and the animals had all escaped!

Wainey got caught up in the string.

I grabbed one end of the
string and gave a big yank!

Wainey went spinning
away like a top.

He whirled through the house, crashing into things and bouncing off.

The gerbils fell out of a vase...

and I caught them.

The hamster was knocked
from a potted palm.

The rabbit was hurled
from a bookcase.

I caught the turtle...and nabbed the parakeet as it flew by.
But just when I had all the animals back..."

"Each one landed in its own place!

Just then the neighbors arrived."